For Faye - S.P.
For my Mother - SB

MYRIAD BOOKS LIMITED
35 Bishopsthorpe Road, London SE26 4PA

First published in 1992 by
FRANCES LINCOLN LIMITED
4 Torriano Mews
Torriano Avenue
London NW5 2RZ

ISBN 1 84746 042 9
EAN 9 781 84746 042 4

Printed in China

Little Bird

Saviour Pirotta
Illustrated by **Stephen Butler**

MYRIAD BOOKS LIMITED

"What can I do today?" asked the little bird.

"Hop," said the bug.

"Wriggle," said the worm.

"Jump," said the frog.

"Bristle," said the hedgehog.

"Paddle," said the duck.

"Skip," said the lamb.

"Roll," said the pig.

"Gallop," said the horse.

"Munch," said the cow.

"Fly," said the little bird's mother. "Fly".

So the little bird flew. All around the farm, right across the fields.

And got back home
just in time for bed.